Leo,
The Fearless and Furless Lion

by Dyeneka Campa

Dedication

To the children who have yet to discover the beauty of their language, hair texture, or complexion ...

This is for you.

The roads are sprinkled with big orange and yellow leaves, and the wind is cool. Leo peeks through the kitchen window after he pours cold milk on his breakfast cereal.

"Oh, I am so excited to go back to school!"

He takes one last spoonful and heads out the door.

1

Leo happens to see his dear friend Sandy, the brightest sunflower in town while walking down the road.

"Morning, Leo! Have a great day at school!"

Leo responds, "Thanks, Sandy. See you later!" as he bounces his basketball and hurries down the road.

3

4

The teacher, Mrs. Ostrich, welcomes all her new students and says, "Please say 'here' when I call your name."

"Rachel Rabbit?"
"Here!"
"Freddy Fox?"
"Here!"
"Leo Lion?" . . .

Mrs. Ostrich looks around the room and repeats again, "Leo LioOoOon?"

5

6

Suddenly, Leo runs in and says,

"RwwAaawright here, Mrs. Ostrich!"

but….

everyone in class starts laughing.
"HaHAhaha, HeheHEhe".

8

9

Leo looks left. . . Leo looks right.

Leo can now see that each of his classmates look very different from last year.

The turtle has a big, strong, green shell.
The elephant has pearly-white, ivory tusks.
The bird has fluffy, vibrant, colorful feathers.

But Leo's lion mane had not grown in yet, and everyone in class expects a lion to have a mane.

Leo's cheeks turn pink because he is feeling very embarrassed.

Leo remains quiet for the rest of class while staring at the clock, counting the minutes until recess.

The recess bell finally rings! Leo is especially eager to escape the classroom, so he grabs his basketball and races to the court to play a game or two.

16

Wesley the weasel, the best basketball player in school, sees Leo walking towards the court to play, but he stops him before he takes a single step further.

"Well, look who we have here, it's Leo, the little lion without his mane, and he wants to play basketball with the big boys. What do you think guys?"

18

The weasels shake their heads and say,

"Tell that little lion to go play in the kiddie sandbox with the kindergarteners, HAhaHa!"

They walk away and continue playing without Leo.

20

Leo is feeling very sad he cannot play.

He takes a seat at the nearby bench all by himself for the rest of recess.

22

The school day is over, and Leo begins walking home. He looks up once he hears his dear friend Sandy the sunflower say,

"Hey, Leo! You don't look so happy. Is everything okay?"

Leo explains to Sandy that he feels down because all his classmates made fun of him because he hasn't grown in his mane yet. Sandy tells Leo to cheer up because she has an idea up her sleeve.

24

Leo soon arrives at Mr. Giraffe's costume store,
the perfect place in town to explore.
He looks around and decides to try on some
items for fun.

"This one is too itchy!"

"This one is too colorful!"

26

"This one is too heavy, WhaOoOoah!"

Leo decides it is best to ask Mr. Giraffe for some help.

"I need something big, wild, and furry. Something perfect for a lion."

Mr. Giraffe says, "Hmm, ah ha! I have just the thing!"

28

Mr. Giraffe stretches his neck to the very top shelf and picks a big, wild, furry lion mane.

Leo yells, "Perfect!"

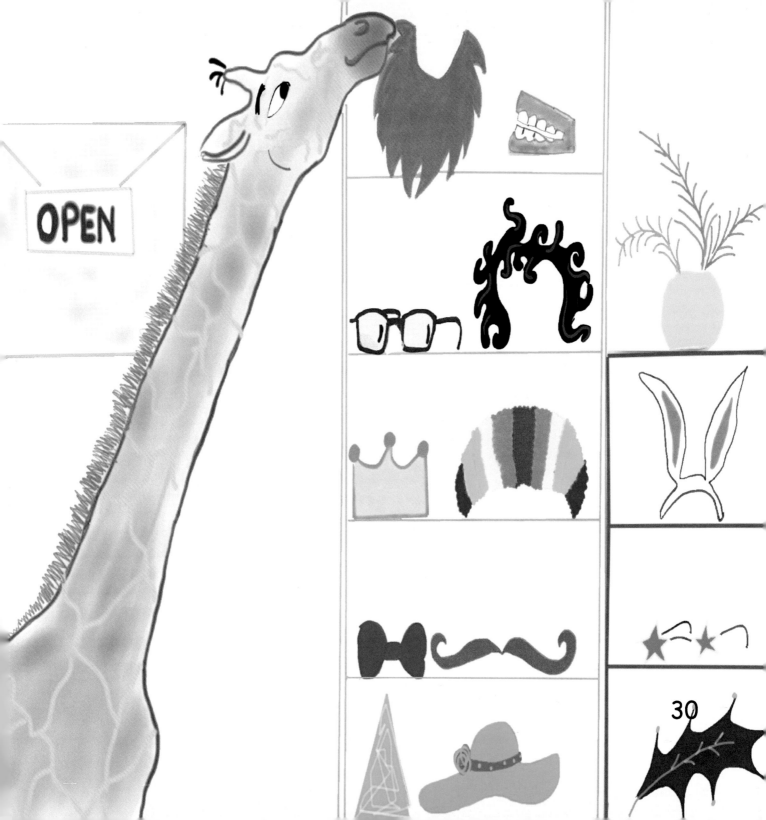

OPEN

30

Leo heads home very happy and excited to wear his new lion mane tomorrow at school.

32

"Leo, is that you?"

Sandy says to Leo while he is on his way to school.

"Wow, you look great!"

Leo stops and playfully fluffs his new mane for Sandy.

"Ah, gee thanks, Sandy! Wish me luck!"

34

Leo finally makes it to class, and not a single classmate recognizes him. Even Mrs. Ostrich thinks Leo is a brand-new student in class.

"Oh, why hello there dear, please introduce yourself to the class."

Leo nervously clears his throat and says,

"Su-su-sure. Hi everyone, my name is Le... I mean, Jasper. My name is Jasper!"

36

Leo looks left. Leo looks right.
All of his classmates are smiling and excited to
meet him.

38

As Leo walks outside for recess he hears Wesley the weasel say,

"Hey, it's that new lion in class. You wanna play a game with us?"

"Sure! My name is Jasper, by the way" Leo quickly says as he runs onto the court and plays with the weasels.

40

It was an exciting game during recess. Leo caught every pass, made every shot, and ran faster than anyone else. The whole team of weasels were very impressed with his skills.

"Look at Jasper go!" one weasel yells during the game.

41

Leo has become the most popular kid in class this week. Everyone wants to play with Leo during recess, have him as a partner for group work time, and even share their favorite snacks with him.

Leo really enjoys being Jasper, the lion who is liked by everyone at school.

44

It's finally Friday, the last day of the week. Leo and the weasels are having a blast on the court. With only a few minutes left, Leo goes for a slam dunk.

And. . and. . .

"SwoOoOoosh!" He makes it
in!

46

Leo lands on both feet and screams,
"Woo hoo! Now that's a slam dunk!"

. . .But everyone goes silent.

48

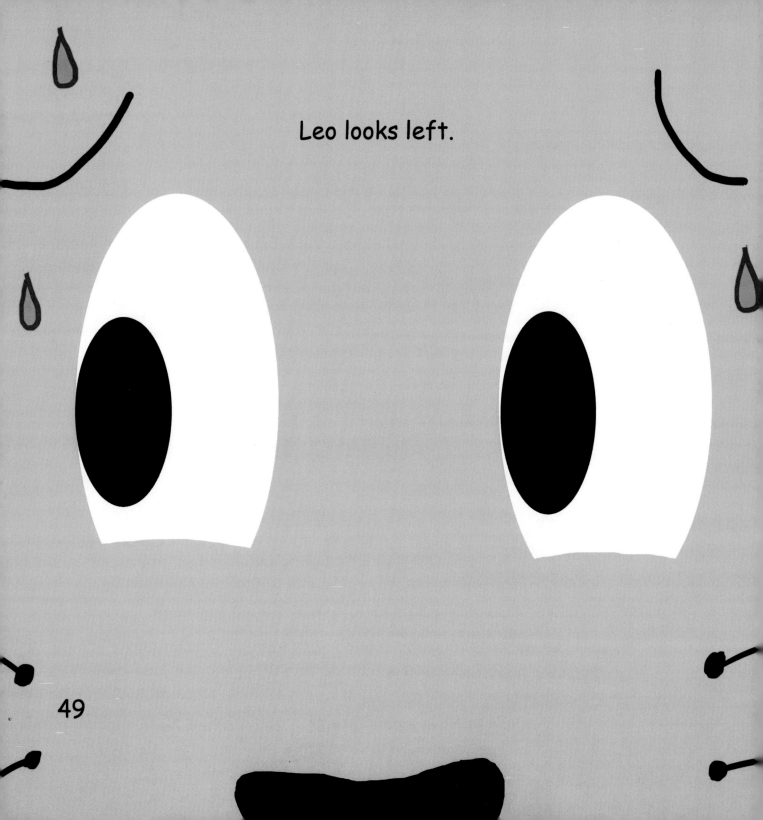

Leo looks left.

49

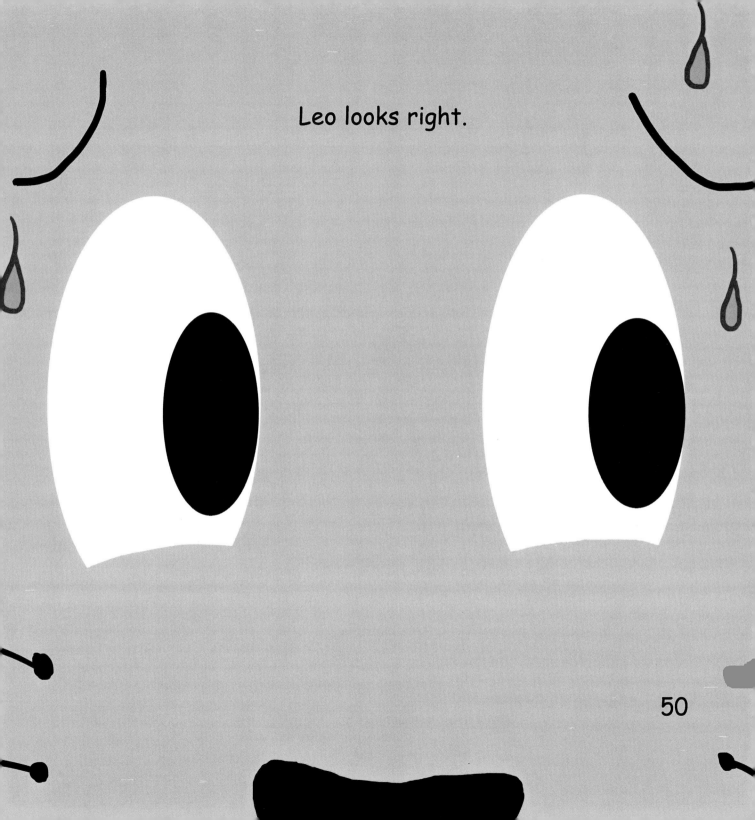

Leo looks right.

50

But then, Leo looks down.

"Oh no!"

Leo gasps. His mane has fallen off his face, and everyone is now laughing at him, just like the first day of school. "Hahaha! Hehehe!" Wesley the weasel says, "Wait, you're not Jasper. You're that one lion without his mane! You're Furless Leo! The little itty-bitty lion haha!"

53

54

For a whole week, Leo was liked by everyone and most of all, he fit in because he was Jasper. Leo then thinks to himself,
"But, it doesn't matter if I have mane or not because I am still the same lion."

56

Leo kicks the mane to the side of the court and says,

"I am a lion no matter if I have a mane or not!

"You should be able to beat me in a game of one on one if I am just a little itty-bitty lion, Wesley. How about that?"

Wesley laughs and passes the basketball to Leo. "Challenge accepted!"

Like lightning, Leo bolts down the court with
all of his might.

62

He jumps from the floor into the air soaring like a bird as he tosses the basketball into the hoop.

And . . . And. . .

64

HE MAKES IT IN!

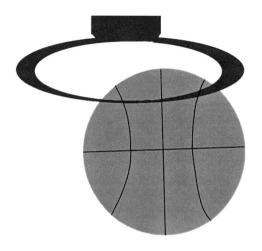

66

Everyone at the court cheers for Leo, including Wesley! Leo is just as good as anybody else in class; it does not matter that he looks different.

68

All the kids looked left. All the kids looked right. Everyone realizes that they are all different, unique, and special in their own way.

70

For the rest of the year, Leo went to school being the best way he could, not as Jasper, but as himself. Leo the Fearless, Furless Lion.

Made in the USA
San Bernardino, CA
09 December 2017